RACE THE WILD

OUTBACK ALL-STARS

RACE THE WILD

ARE YOU READY TO RUN THE WILDEST RACE OF YOUR LIFE?

RACE THE WILD

OUTBACK ALL-STARS

·BY **KRISTIN EARHART**·
·ILLUSTRATED BY **ERWIN MADRID**·

SCHOLASTIC INC.

TO MY DAD, WHO iS A REAL WORLD-CiRCLiNG JET-SETTER —KJE

Text copyright © 2016 by Kristin Earhart.
Illustrations copyright © 2016 by Scholastic Inc.

ISBN 978-0-545-94064-1

10 9 8 7 6 5 4 3 2 1   16 17 18 19 20

Printed in the U.S.A.   40
First printing 2016

Book design by Yaffa Jaskoll

CHAPTER 1

ALL-STAR EXTRAVAGANZA

"**I** wonder what we're in for this time . . ."

Sage Stevens recognized the voice as soon as she heard it. She could identify it even with the blindfold on. Russell Dean! She was glad he was there. She had only met Russell six months earlier, but he was a loyal teammate and friend. The Wild Life organizers might be trying to keep the contestants in the dark, with the blindfolds and all, but at least she could count on Russell being on her team.

"Hi, Russell," she said as her escorts led her into a tent. "Who else is here?"

Sage couldn't believe she was back for another race. She felt the familiar tightness in her stomach, the rush at the thought of competition. Still blindfolded, she turned to one of the guides who had directed her to the tent. He was fumbling with the knot at the back of her head. "I can get it. Thanks," she announced, swatting the clumsy hands away.

In a smooth motion, Sage reached up, easily loosened the sweaty blindfold, and placed it in the hands of the dazed guide. She brushed her blonde hair from her face and then faced the three kids gathered in the dim light of the camping tent.

"Team Red!" she exclaimed. "Dev!" She reached up for a high five. It had been four months since

she'd seen any of her old teammates. Dev Patel looked taller, but the tech-wiz was just as skinny.

"Russell," Sage stated solemnly, a smirk tugging at the side of her mouth.

"Sage," he answered, giving her hand a firm, dignified shake. Sage squeezed as hard as she could. Russell tried to stay serious, but his face erupted in a radiant smile, his teeth a bright white against his dark skin.

"Show-off," Russell said. "What? You been lifting weights?"

"Maybe," Sage answered with a shrug, even though she hadn't. But she suspected Russell might have. Between baseball, track, and football, he was always training for something.

Next, Sage turned to Mari Soto, the final and most essential member of Team Red. Mari looked pretty much the same. Her hair was still in a single, long braid. Her eyes were still a soft, warm brown.

"Hi, Sage." Mari's voice was quiet, but she stepped forward and wrapped her thin arms around Sage with impressive force.

"Hi, Mari," Sage answered, giving Mari's back a gentle pat.

It was obvious they were the same four kids. Sage wondered if they still had the same "stuff" that had made them a great team. They'd all been strangers six months ago, but they had somehow come together to conquer all of the other teams in the tenth running of *The Wild Life*, an around-the-world race through the animal kingdom.

But that was last summer. Now it was winter break, and the Wild Life organizers had decided they wanted a best-of-the-best competition—an all-star extravaganza. Team Red—Mari, Russell, Dev, and Sage—had been invited back. This time, the prize was even better: one million dollars for the team and one million dollars for the team's favorite charity. Plus, the winners got to take their families on a true safari. With track season over, Sage was thrilled to have another race ahead of her.

They would be pitted against other winning teams from past races. "Do we know who the competition is yet?" Sage asked.

"Nope," Russell replied. "Remember the blindfolds?"

"We don't know much," Dev added. "We only have this note. And it isn't even a real clue."

Reunited — together again,

But not complete.

Soon you will have

The missing piece that

Will help you to compete.

"A missing piece?" Sage repeated, doubt in her voice.

"Maybe it's the ancam," Dev suggested. Of course Dev mentioned the device that all teams used to communicate with the organizers of the race. It had been how they had received all of their clues—and how they had submitted their photos and answers. Dev had always been in charge of it for the team.

"So we know nothing," Sage concluded.

"Except that we're back in Australia," Mari pointed out.

"And we can be sure they won't send us to the reef, since we were just there," added Russell.

Sage agreed with that. Team Red had spent an entire leg of their race just off the shore of Australia in the Great Barrier Reef. It had been amazing, but the Wild Life organizers wouldn't go back there so soon. "Any idea where we're headed then?" Sage asked, looking again at Mari.

It wasn't as if the other girl had inside information. What Mari had was better than that. Sage called it "animal intuition." Back in the African savanna, Mari had predicted one of the key questions in the race. Sage hoped she would do that again.

"I have no idea," Mari answered with a shrug.

"This is All-Stars. We don't even know if the clues will work the same way." Mari pulled off the rubber band at the end of her braid and ran her hands through her long, dark hair. Absentmindedly, she began to divide it into sections and twist it into a tight, neat braid again. "Of course," she said after a while, "the koala lives only on the eastern side of the continent."

"Really?" Russell questioned. "I thought they lived all over. There were koalas on tons of the postcards at the airport."

"Nope," Mari confirmed with an exacting shake of her head. "They live along the coast, on some islands, and in forests, but all on the eastern side. I know it seems obvious, but I'll bet there's a clue for them early in the race, before we head inland."

"Yes!" Sage exclaimed. "I knew you'd get us thinking on the right track, Mari. Everyone, start thinking of koala facts."

But Mari was just getting started. "There are lots of other awesome marsupials that live in the eastern rain forests," Mari added. "And we can't forget the mountain heath dragon."

"Oh, yes. Of course. The mountain heath dragon," Dev mocked. "How could we forget that?"

Mari shot him a playful scowl. She opened her mouth, ready to add other animals to the list, when the tent flap lifted. The two guides who had escorted Sage into the tent stood there.

"Team Red, Season 10," the one with a beard said, tapping an electronic pad with his finger.

"You got it," Russell confirmed. "That's us."

"When you get outside, look for your banner on the left."

The other guide pulled a slender gadget from a canvas bag. He handed it to Dev.

"All right," Dev murmured, running his fingers across the keyboard. "Another ancam upgrade."

Sage led the group out of the tent. They were in some kind of outdoor theater with a stage down in front. Tall trees grew on either side. There were two rows of long wooden benches. Sage recognized teams from previous seasons already in their seats. It was crowded. This was going to be a full field of contestants.

Just as she located the banner that marked Team Red, Season 10's spot, she noticed a line of people on the stage. But they weren't just any people. They were former contestants.

"What are they doing here?" Russell whispered over Sage's shoulder.

"I don't know," Sage admitted, and she wasn't sure she wanted to find out.

MARVELOUS MARSUPIALS

WALLABY

JOEY

Marsupials are a special group of animals. All marsupials are mammals, which means they have hair and produce milk to feed their young. Most marsupials also have a marsupium, which is a fancy name for a pouch.

Marsupial babies are called joeys. The joeys are tiny, blind, and hairless when they are born.

Barely the size of a jelly bean, a marsupial baby crawls into its mother's pouch as soon as it is born. There, it can drink milk and stay safe and warm. It will not come out until it is much bigger, several weeks—or even months—later. While the famous kangaroo and koala usually only have one baby at a time, many marsupials have litters of three or more.

People often think of Australia as the land of marsupials. Because Australia is far away from other continents, many kinds of marsupials live there and nowhere else. Australia has about two hundred different species of marsupials! While Central and South America together have about 70 marsupial species, North America is home to only one: the Virginia opossum.

CHAPTER 2

OLD RIVALS, REUNITED

"**W**hy is Dallas up there?" Dev asked Russell.

"And Eliza," Mari added. Ten kids sat on the raised stage. The two sitting directly in front of Team Red's banner were Dallas and Eliza—Team Red's top rivals from the last race. It hardly seemed like a coincidence.

"How should I know why they're here?" Russell answered, his voice tense. He sat down, slumped forward, and folded his hands over his head.

"Dallas didn't say anything to you?" Sage

prompted in a hushed voice. She took the spot next to Russell on the wooden bench.

"No, I swear," Russell replied. He turned to look at Sage. "We haven't talked about *The Wild Life* at all. I thought that was a good thing."

Sage thought Russell was probably right. He had known Dallas and the other boys on the green team from home. And when Team Green had tried to cheat, Russell had refused to turn in his old friends. Knowing the truth, Sage didn't like seeing Dallas on stage. But if it didn't feel right to her, she imagined it made Russell felt even worse.

As she sat on the bench, she felt an odd tingling feeling, like something crawling on her back. When she looked up, she realized that Eliza was staring her down. During the previous race, Eliza had made it clear that if it were a battle of the brains, her team should have won. But *The Wild Life* didn't work that way.

Sage locked eyes with the other girl until Bull Gordon strode down the aisle. As always, the popular host of the competition commanded everyone's attention.

"Hello, racers!" Bull's voice boomed as he climbed the steps to the stage. He wore his trademark hat, a fedora with a jagged shark's tooth tucked in the band. He looked ready for adventure. "It's good to see you all." A broad smile stretched across his face.

"Onstage are some of *The Wild Life*'s strongest contestants," Bull continued, turning to the group seated behind him. "They're the best competitors we've seen in all ten seasons of the race. But none of these players actually won." Sage focused on

Dallas and Eliza. "That's about to change. One of these former contestants will join each team, so everyone on the stage will get a second chance to win it all. Believe me, former winners, you will appreciate another team member. You're going to need all the help you can get! Now, there will be two legs of the race." The host paused and held up two fingers. "The first takes place here, in Australia, and it includes two very different habitats. As of now, we have ten teams, but be warned: Some of you will be eliminated at the halfway point! Only the top teams will move on to the second habitat."

The members of Team Red exchanged uncertain glances. There were going to be early eliminations? That had never happened before. And a new member would join their team? Sage glanced up at the stage and quickly considered the possibilities. It would be cool if they got someone from one of the first seasons; that person would be older, probably stronger, and possibly smarter. Sage immediately saw two interesting possibilities: a tall girl with broad shoulders and spazzy curls; and a guy dressed like a professional mountain climber but with chunky glasses and spiked hair. Sage thought either of them might be a good addition to their team.

But she soon learned the teams wouldn't get to choose. "You will draw names from a hat to select your new team member," Bull announced. At that point, a familiar face appeared onstage, carrying an upside-down hat in his hands.

"Javier!" Mari gasped. Javier had been Team Red's chaperone on their first race. Everyone loved him. Javier flashed the group an easy smile, but then his expression quickly clouded. Sage assumed it was because it was time to grab team-mates out of a hat.

"We will go in order," explained Bull. "The team from Season 1 will pick first. Season 2 second, and so on."

"So we're last," Russell mumbled.

"Yep," Sage answered with a heavy sigh. Sage hated waiting. But she hated not being in control even more. If they had to have another member, Sage wished it could be her sister, Caroline. After all, the two sisters had at first planned to run the race together. But that hadn't worked out. Sage had a feeling this wouldn't, either.

The teams picked names and, one by one, all the older contestants were selected.

"This is a joke, right?" Dev said when there were just two contestants left. "We're stuck with Miss Know-It-All or Mister I-Cheat-Off-My-Best-Friends?"

Sage couldn't believe it, either. Eliza and Dallas were the only two remaining racers. For a moment, she didn't know which option was worse. Eliza had been the leader of Team Purple. She was smart, but bossy. Sage did not see them being friends.

Sage glanced at Russell. He was hunched over, his forehead pressed against his hands. No way could Russell deal with being on the same team as Dallas.

Sage looked up at the stage where Vincent, the leader of Season 9, was about to pick a name from the fedora.

"Dallas Hughes!" Bull called out.

Dallas leapt from his seat and fist-bumped Vincent. He immediately put his arm around the team leader like they had always been friends.

"Season 10, last but not least," Bull stated. "Come on up."

Sage put her hand on Russell's shoulder as she walked by. Like all the other team leaders, Sage climbed up to the stage. It was no surprise when she saw Eliza Zwilling's name on the slip of paper she pulled from Javier's hat. Sage smiled with relief. Eliza was way better than Dallas and "all that baggage," as her grandmother would say.

Eliza rushed up to Sage. "I could tell you guys wanted me. I was holding out for you, too," Eliza whispered, even though Bull was the only one who could possibly hear. "We're going to do great. I've literally read a hundred books about

Australian habitats. You'll be glad you have me to help you lead this team."

Sage gritted her teeth. They had not needed Eliza to win the previous race, and Sage doubted they needed her now.

"All-Stars, your teams are complete," Bull Gordon announced. "You are all veterans. You may have raced before, but you must always remember to show respect for all that surrounds you, even one another. That is essential to competing in *The Wild Life*." The host paused and examined the audience once more. "Return to your tents, and keep your ancams handy. You'll need them before you know it."

Sage looked up at the sunset-painted sky as she and Eliza joined Team Red. The sun was going down, but it looked like the race was just heating up.

AUSTRALIA

AUSTRALIA'S NATURAL REGIONS

- EQUATORIAL
- TROPICAL
- SUBTROPICAL
- DESERT
- SAVANNA
- TEMPERATE

Is it a country or a continent? Both! While it is the world's smallest continent, Australia is the sixth largest country.

Australia is home to many amazing creatures. Over half the plants and animals there are endemic to Australia. *Endemic* means that they are special to a place; those plants and animals do not live naturally in the wild anywhere else.

The center of Australia is very dry and flat. (This area is often called the Outback.) There are also green forests in the mountains as well as pockets of lush rain forests all over the continent. This variety of climates allows for a great variety of plants and animals. Australia boasts some of the most exotic creatures in the world. It also has water on all sides, so there are lots of beaches with aquatic wildlife, like turtles and fish.

CHAPTER 3

NIGHT IS RIGHT

"We're striking out now, at night?" Russell's backpack shifted as he double knotted his high-tops. They had returned to the tent to find a pile of backpacks already loaded with clothes and gear. And a map marked with an X. "It's pitch-black out! Do they want to get the All-Stars killed?"

"I can't answer that," Dev admitted. "But I can tell you that the ancam is my master, and it says we are allowed to leave the tent in four and a half minutes."

"We leave the second it tells us we can," Sage stated. She didn't care about the darkness. She just wanted to get started. "It's not like we'd be able to sleep now anyway," Sage pointed out. "I'm ready to race."

"That's no surprise," said Russell.

"I'm ready, too," declared Eliza.

Sage glanced over at the newest member of Team Red. Despite. the fact that they were all wearing almost the exact same thing—a red T-shirt and army-green cargo shorts—Eliza's uniform looked as if she'd packed a travel iron to get rid of the wrinkles. And ever since Bull Gordon had announced her name, she'd had an eager smile pasted on her face, like she was posing for a school picture. Sage decided that the caption underneath would say ELIZA ZWILLING: SUPER PROUD TO BE A SUPER SMARTIE.

Eliza adjusted the straps on her backpack so they were exactly even on both sides. "What are you wearing?" she asked Dev, motioning to the harness strapped across his chest.

"You like it? It's my ancam clasp," Dev said, straightening up to show off the contraption. Then, in one smooth motion, he whipped out the ancam and had it in ready position. His pointer finger was prepared to punch keys. "My mom and I made it." His eyebrows shot up when he grinned. "You never know. The race could come down to a few important seconds, so you have to be fast."

"Oh, I know," Eliza murmured, her eyes squinting.

Sage could tell Eliza was still holding a grudge. She couldn't blame her. Team Red had slipped right past Team Purple on the final clue. Team Red had won, fair and square, but if the roles had been reversed, Sage would be annoyed, too.

Mari had been busy braiding her hair one last time. As soon as she snapped the rubber band in place, she stood up, instantly alert. "It makes sense that we're heading out in the dark," she noted. "Over half of Australia's mammals are marsupials, and most of them are active at night."

"They're nocturnal. That's the scientific word," Eliza said. "And some are crepuscular, which means they are active both in the morning and evening."

The four original members of Team Red looked at one another, but Eliza didn't notice. She was still going over vocabulary words. "But, Mari, there is one exception. The numbat is diurnal. That means it is only active during the day. It is the only Australian diurnal marsupial."

Mari pursed her lips and nodded. "You're right."

"I know," Eliza answered.

Sage was relieved when she heard rustling at the front of the tent. The bearded guide from earlier poked his head inside. "Almost ready, Team Ten?" he asked.

Sage gave the tent and her team a quick glanc "Sure thing," she answered.

"Of course," Eliza said at the same time

Sage gave a half-hearted smile. "Is Jav ing?" she wondered, trying to look pas to see if their old chaperone was ap

"Oh," the bearded guide said, "Javier is paired with Season 9. I'm Jace."

Sage, Russell, Mari, and Dev were silent.

"Hi, Jace," Eliza announced, her hand extended. "I'm Eliza. I want to be the first to thank you for being our chaperone on *The Wild Life: Outback All-Stars*."

The others quickly came forward and greeted the new guide. He seemed nice enough. "Oh, and another thing," he said. "You're now Team Ten. We had three Team Reds and two Team Blues, so we're numbering by season now."

Dev shrugged. "Ten's a good number," he said.

"At least we still get to wear red," Russell offered.

Then Team Ten left the tent and entered the

night. Out of the corner of her eye, Sage caught sight of Javier.

The beam from Javier's headlamp lingered on his old team for a moment. He raised his hand. Sage smiled and waved back. Only as she turned away did she spot Dallas Hughes, the newest member of Team Nine.

Dev and Sage led the group, sharing the map so they could locate the best path to the X. They soon realized that each group must have a different destination. There were ten teams, and each one was heading down a different trail away from the tents.

"Let's pick up the pace," Sage called once they had separated from the other teams. With her headlamp tilted down, she took off at a steady

jog. She kept her eyes on the ground to avoid roots or rocks that could trip them up. Tree branches arched overhead, blocking any view of the moon or stars. The path was steep, but Sage pushed harder through the muggy air.

The night seemed quiet until a low growl filled the forest.

"What was that?" Russell asked.

Sage didn't know. She had never heard anything like it. She felt hundreds of goose bumps spring up on her arms and neck, but she forged ahead. "Just keep moving," she said, suddenly aware that her heart was pounding.

The bellow came again.

She kept up the pace until the wide path forked into two narrow trails. "What now?" she wondered, listening for another growl.

"This is it." Dev was already on the ancam. "I punched in our location," he said. "And now we've got our clue." He read it out loud.

Ursus, it is not.
The nickname's all wrong.
A two-thumbed tree dweller,
With a call more grunt than song.

CREATURE FEATURE

KOALA

SCIENTIFIC NAME: *Phascolarctos cinereus*

TYPE: mammal

RANGE: southeastern Australia

FOOD: leaves, primarily of one of many species of eucalyptus

Part of the koala's scientific name comes from two Greek words meaning "pouch bear." The koala does have a pouch, but it is not closely related to bears at all. It is a marsupial, and a very fluffy, cuddly-looking one at that. Despite its sweet face, the koala can be aggressive. Male koalas are ferocious when fighting for territory.

As with many animals, the koala's life revolves around getting food. The koala's favorite is eucalyptus leaves. It is an interesting choice, because eucalyptus is toxic enough to make a person sick. A koala, however, has developed an ability to digest it. While still in the pouch, the baby eats its mother's pap. *Pap* is already-digested eucalyptus, and eating it makes it easier for the baby koala to one day digest the fresh leaves, too. Eucalyptus provides little energy, so the koala rests about nineteen hours a day. Of the five hours it is active, at least three are for eating more eucalyptus.

CHAPTER 4

GROWL OR BURP?

Sage's mind whirled as she tried to match the hints in the clue with animal facts she knew.

"Well, that's really easy," Eliza declared. "As usual, I can get it from the first line. *Ursus* is a scientific word for bear, but the clue says that the animal is not a bear. So it's obviously the koala. Everyone knows the koala isn't a bear."

A small part of Sage wanted to point out to Eliza that the team already had a Smartie who knew everything about animals. They didn't need her to recite facts from her encyclopedias, but Sage didn't say anything. Eliza was on their team now. Sage would just have to figure out what else Eliza could contribute.

When no one responded, Eliza kept going. "The koala lives in trees and has two thumbs for gripping branches. And the books say that a koala's call is very low."

As if on cue, the growl they'd heard earlier once again filled the night.

"Was that a koala?" Sage asked.

"Well, yeah," Eliza answered, but she didn't look so sure.

The call came once more, this time longer and lower. The deep snarl was followed by a gruff gulping sound.

"It's like half growl and half burp," Dev said with a shudder.

"That doesn't sound like a koala," Russell insisted. "It sounds like a monster that eats kids in the dark." He glanced around, shooting his headlamp beam in all directions.

"This isn't a video game," Sage reminded Russell. Yet his comment didn't seem far off. How could a little koala make such a deep sound? She glanced at Jace. He did not look concerned. Sage assumed if they were in real danger, he'd let them know.

"Actually, koalas have an extra voice organ that helps them make that sound," Mari explained. "Most animals that make big, deep sounds are large, like gorillas or elephants. But the koala is special." Mari's voice trailed off as she slipped away from the group. She stepped off the path and gazed into the trees. The answer to the clue was clearly a koala, but they had to get a picture of one in order to move on to the next stage of the race.

"The bellow came from back there," Eliza said.

Mari's head tilted to one side as she stared upward. The trees were tall and slender with leaves to match. Sage recognized them as eucalyptus. She knew it was the favorite food of most koalas. Mari moved farther into the thick of the forest.

Eliza stood on the edge of the path, eyeing Mari. "You do know that Australia has more venomous snakes than any other continent? You shouldn't just wander off."

Mari just stood still and listened.

"Twenty-one of the twenty-five deadliest snake species to be exact," Eliza added. "So maybe we should stay on the path."

"We could do that, but I think Dev would get a better shot from here," Mari said, gesturing toward a tree just over her head.

"Really?" Dev questioned.

"Really," Mari confirmed.

"Don't let that koala go anywhere!" Dev joined Mari and aimed the ancam. The flash illuminated the deep-green canopy of trees. "Look, she has a joey in her pouch."

The teammates crowded together to get a peek at the tiny koala.

Sage was amazed that Mari could have even seen the koala. Its gray fur blended in with the bark of the tree.

The mom blinked when the light of their head-lamps hit her eyes. She looked just like all of the postcards: black pebble-shaped nose, white fluff in her ears, thick claws on her double thumbs.

"Nice work, Mari," Sage said, feeling the same sense of awe she had during their first race together. "But that was almost too easy. It's like they dropped us right in the middle of a koala colony. I'll bet the other teams were lucky, too. Let's keep moving."

"Here's the next clue," said Dev.

```
High-pitched echoes

I cannot hear.

But I can smell food out

With my super snout.

Flower or fig,

My appetite is mega-big.
```

Sage was sure she could get this one. Eliza might be a know-it-all, but she was also right. The first line had a huge hint, and so did the last line.

"They keep telling us what the animal isn't," Dev pointed out. "Or what it can't do. Those are big clues."

"So if it can't hear high-pitched echoes," Russell said, "it isn't hunting with echolocation, right? That's when bats send out sounds and wait for the echoes to bounce back to figure out where things are. Lots of bats use it to find their insect dinners."

"Exactly. But it could still be a bat even if it doesn't use echolocation," Sage said. "And they used the word 'mega,' which refers to a kind of bat."

"Yes. It refers to the fruit bats or bats that eat fruit," Eliza said with an exacting clip. "As you should know, mega means big, and most fruit bats are bigger than the insect eaters. They're also called flying foxes, because their heads look a lot like—"

"—a pirate ship," Dev cut in. Sage smirked. She could tell he was joking, but Eliza looked surprised by the interruption.

"Okay," Sage said. "So we know they look like foxes. Do we all agree that we are looking for a fruit bat?"

"Yes," the other four members answered.

"Has anyone seen any?" Sage asked. "Because they're probably not going to just sit around like the koala."

Dev was holding up the ancam, playing with the settings. "Maybe we can catch one eating. Otherwise, we'll need to get up higher, so we can see them in the open sky."

When Sage gazed above her, she could barely see beyond the reach of her arm. The leaves cloaked the forest in darkness. They had been lucky finding the koala so quickly. It wouldn't be as easy with a bat.

CREATURE FEATURE

GREY-HEADED FLYING FOX

SCIENTIFIC NAME: *Pteropus poliocephalus*

TYPE: mammal

RANGE: southeastern Australia

FOOD: blossoms, nectar, and fruit

The scientific order that includes all bats is Chiroptera. It means "hand-wing." The name refers to the fact that the bones in the wing are very similar to those of a hand.

Bats are separated into two groups: microbats and megabats. While "micro" and "mega" refer to size, these names can be confusing. Not all megabats are larger than microbats. A better way to tell them apart is by their food. Microbats usually eat insects, and most megabats feast on flowers and fruit. There are physical differences that reflect the way they hunt, too. Microbats use their ears to hear echoes, so their ears are larger and adapted to this skill. Megabats rely more on sight and smell. Therefore, they have larger eyes and noses.

"Flying fox" is another term for megabat. The grey-headed flying fox is one of the largest bats in the world. While their bodies are roughly a foot long, their wingspan can reach five feet. Their heads, with an obvious snout, do resemble that of a fox. The grey-headed flying fox even has a stylish ruffle of rust-colored fur around its neck. Very foxy.

CHAPTER 5

UP IN THE AIR

"Maybe we should stop and listen," Eliza suggested. "I read that some flying foxes have over thirty different calls. We might hear them."

"Do you know what they sound like?" Russell asked.

"Not exactly," admitted Eliza. "But I think we should explore every possibility. Or maybe you have a better idea?"

Eliza was pushy, but Sage knew she had a point. "We can give it a try," she said. "It can't hurt."

Sage watched Eliza and Mari close their eyes. Then she caught Russell and Dev rolling theirs. Sage glared at them until they did the same. As soon as Sage's eyes were closed, the forest's sounds were magnified. Everything was louder. She could hear life in many forms: rustling, scurrying, squawking, chewing. But Sage could not be certain she heard a bat. She did, however, hear people.

When Sage opened her eyes, Eliza was right in front of her. The other girl held a very straight finger up to her lips. She motioned to the group and directed them into the shadows.

"What are we doing?" Sage asked, but Eliza just raised her finger again. This time, she pointed with it.

A mass of dark figures crossed overhead. "Do you see that?" Eliza asked, her words fast and precise. "It's a walkway that takes you up into the canopy. That's where we need to be."

Sage remembered that the canopy was the top level of a rain forest. It was in the highest branches of the tallest trees. During the day, the sunlight reached that level, so it thrived with life. "How do we get up there?" Sage whispered.

The straight finger returned. This time, a stern scowl came with it. Eliza motioned and led the way.

Sage wondered how many teams were ahead of them. If the organizers were going to eliminate some teams early, Sage had to make sure her team wasn't one of them.

With a twist around an enormous fig tree, and a turn past a grove of lush palm trees, Eliza delivered the team to what looked like a secret spiral staircase. It wrapped around a giant tree trunk as it went up, up, up.

"If we're going to find a fruit bat, this is the way to do it," Dev said.

"Watch out for snakes," Eliza whispered over her shoulder. "Most of them can climb. There's the common tree snake, the brown tree snake, and all the pythons. The pythons are constrictors, which means they squeeze their prey to death."

Sage flinched as she smacked into a branch that reached over the winding staircase. She shoved the leaves out of the way and climbed to the top. As she left the staircase behind, the thick cover of leaves gave way to the starry sky above. The walkway had a railing, but Sage still felt exposed. Up in the trees, the air was cooler. It whirled around on all sides, making Sage uncertain of her next step in the dark.

Dev strode out to a platform that jutted out over the forest. Below, a waterfall dropped into a rocky pool with crystal-clear splashes. It was breathtaking, but Sage was concerned. Why were they the only team there? It was a prime view. Had all the other teams already moved on?

"I see something!" Russell called out in a dramatic whisper. It took a moment for her eyes to adjust, but Sage soon focused in on a graceful form, swooping through the sky. "It's flying, right over there."

"It's a sugar glider," Mari said. "And it's not actually flying. Just watch."

Sure enough, the creature soared downward through the air but soon landed on a tree trunk.

"Did you see how its *wings* disappeared as soon as it gripped the tree?" Mari asked. "That's because they aren't wings; they're thin pieces of skin that catch the air."

"So that's not our bat," Dev said, putting the ancam back in place.

Only moments later, Dev whipped it out again. "That looks like a bat," he said, holding the ancam up. "But it doesn't seem to be looking for flowers or fruit. It's just dipping and diving."

"That's because it's a microbat," Eliza said. "It's searching for insects. You'll know our mega-bat. It'll be bigger than that."

All at once, they heard a chirping cry.

"Duck!" Russell called out, and the whole team dropped down to their knees.

"That was not a duck," Dev said. "It was a flying fox!" As Dev fumbled with the ancam, Sage watched the bat. Its wingspan looked as wide as her arms. With the moon shining from above, she could almost see through the thin skin that made up the bat's wings. She could spot the map of blood vessels that coursed through them. It was amazing.

"You think this is good enough?" Dev asked, holding up the ancam screen.

"I'm not sure," Russell said. "It looks like a bat, but it doesn't show any of this species' special features."

"It was definitely a grey-headed flying fox," Eliza said. "You could tell by the distinctive rust-colored collar of fur around its neck."

"But you can't see that in the picture," Russell pointed out, frowning at the tiny screen.

"I don't know. Should we risk sending in a not-so-good shot?" Dev wondered.

"I wouldn't worry about it," said Mari as she left the platform and walked back toward the main walkway. "That bat was just leaving its roost, and I think it left something behind."

CREATURE FEATURE

KING BROWN SNAKE

SCIENTIFIC NAME: *Pseudechis australis*

TYPE: reptile

RANGE: most of Australia, except for rain forests and coastal regions in the north, east, and south

FOOD: lizards, birds, frogs, and small mammals

What's in a name? Even though this species has brown and copper-colored scales, it actually belongs to the black snake family. It is Australia's second longest venomous snake, and one of the continent's most dangerous.

The king brown's venom is not overwhelmingly toxic, but it has more of it than most snakes. The longer the snake bites, the more venom that streams into its victim. While snakes do use venom as a form of protection, its main function is for hunting.

Another common name for this species is the mulga snake. A mulga is a kind of short, stubby tree that grows in the dry parts of the country. The term has also come to refer to that open, desertlike land. The king brown snake is called a mulga snake because it thrives in these dry regions, but it also lives in many other climates, except the rain forest.

CHAPTER 6

NO BOATS ABOUT

"Follow Mari," Sage directed, shooing her team-mates with both hands. "And hurry."

Mari stopped at the railing and looked into the thick of the canopy. These trees were home to hundreds of species: mammals, insects, reptiles, amphibians, and birds. Right now, Team Ten was only interested in spotting one.

Mari reached up and angled her headlamp into the gloomy forest. The beam fell on a cluster of bats huddled together, looking cozy even as they hung upside down. The closest one seemed to shudder in the spotlight. "Sorry, little guy," Mari murmured.

Dev leaned into the railing to get a good angle with the ancam.

"They're practically newborns," Mari said. "They're still too young to find food for themselves. They're mammals, so they are probably still drinking milk."

"There are so many of them," Russell commented. The branches were crowded with several small groupings. "They're everywhere."

"It's a colony," Mari confirmed. "Once the babies are a few weeks old, the mothers leave them at the roost when they go out to find food."

"They're so small," Sage noted. "How do we know they're the right type of bat?"

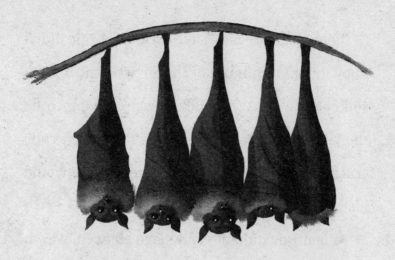

"The small ears," Mari said. "If they hunted with their hearing, their ears would be bigger."

"And their large eyes," Eliza quickly added. "Better for seeing flowers and fruit."

"And the fox-like snout," offered Mari.

"And the fur down to their feet," Eliza said, enunciating each word exactly. "It's a trait special to the grey-headed flying fox."

"And the fact that the race organizers already gave us our next clue," Dev confirmed.

"Thank goodness!" Sage exclaimed. She didn't know how much more of the Smartie showdown she could take. When Eliza wasn't trying to be the leader, she was trying to be the expert code cracker. Sage wished their new teammate would just chill out. "What does it say?"

When Dev did not reply, Sage glanced over at the keeper of the ancam. His forehead was crinkled as he studied the screen. "What is it?" she prompted.

"I'm not sure," he replied. "It reads like this."

```
Over 100 million years ago
Set on its seaward way
This land became its own world.
Many climates it claims today.
```

Now travel to another place
And other clues you'll find.
But if you don't catch your ride
Your quest ends in a bind.

"Clearly it's discussing how Australia came to be on its own, out in the middle of the ocean," Eliza said. "It's hinting at the fact that millions of years ago all the continents were once more or less connected."

"Yes," Mari commented. "And then it mentions the different climates of Australia. So far, we've only seen this one."

"I think we're most concerned with the last two lines," Sage interrupted. "Can you repeat those, Dev?"

After Dev did as Sage asked, he cleared his throat. "And just now a map appeared, with another X marking a spot."

"So, if we don't make it to the X in time, we'll miss our ride and be out of the race?" Sage muttered in disbelief. "That's how they'll eliminate us." She glanced at Jace, who had hardly uttered a word since they had all met in the tent. "How much time do we have? How many teams will make it? What kind of bind?"

Jace shrugged.

At once, the five teammates huddled together, staring at the map. "The map shows this walk-way," Russell pointed out. "And look down there!"

When they gazed over the railing, they saw a team down by the stream. They were getting into a boat.

Team Ten raced to the end of the walkway and scrambled down the stairs, but when they came to the stream, nothing was there.

"Shouldn't there be a boat for us?" Russell asked.

"Did they get the last one?" Mari wondered.

"This should be the place," Dev stated. "Here's a Wild Life marker." He pulled the tip of the flag toward him and let go, so the pole sprung back and forth.

Just then, a low chuckle began to echo through the forest. And then another, and another. The chorus grew to chilling, high-pitched cackles that rang in the air.

"What was that?" Sage asked, searching the shadows above.

"Those are kookaburras," Mari answered.

"They sure find this funny," commented Dev.

"Nothing about this is funny," Sage insisted. She looked to Jace. "So we don't get a boat?"

"I guess the organizers thought this would make things more interesting," the guide said.

"That's just evil," Russell said.

"We're as good as eliminated," Dev concluded.

"So much for my comeback," Eliza mumbled.

"No. We just have to find another way. Let me see that map," Sage demanded. Dev pushed a button that dropped a pin to mark their location.

"We're not even close to the X," Russell said, taking his finger and trailing it along the curvy route suggested by the map. "It'll take forever to get there."

Sage looked again. "But that's if we follow the stream in a boat. What if we cut through the forest on foot?" She took her finger and drew a much straighter line to the X. She looked at Jace again.

"I'm not a cartographer," he said, lifting his hands like he was trying to avoid any blame.

"That means he doesn't draw maps for a living," Eliza informed them.

"I think we got that," Dev told Eliza.

"It's a shortcut," Russell said, still staring at Sage's route on the screen.

"It's a gamble," Dev added.

"It's our best shot," said Sage. She was sure of it.

CREATURE FEATURE

LAUGHING KOOKABURRA

SCIENTIFIC NAME: *Dacelo novaeguineae*

TYPE: bird

RANGE: eastern Australia; it has also been introduced to the southwest corner and Tasmania

FOOD: snakes, lizards, worms, insects, small rodents, snails, and small birds

The kookaburra is not an ordinary songbird. It has a call that starts as a low chuckle, increases to a hearty, high-pitched belly laugh, and ends with another chuckle. Sometimes, other kookaburras will join in the call, making it sound like a rowdy party. It is the way the birds claim territory. The species has other squawks and calls for other purposes, like warning family members of danger, finding a mate, or begging for food.

The family stays in its territory all year and does not migrate. Their home is often a tree hollow in a wet, cool forest.

Although it's a member of the kingfisher family, the kookaburra prefers to eat foods other than fish. Snakes are often at the top of their list. The kookaburra is a skilled hunter. It is strong and stout. It uses its long, spear-shaped bill to catch its prey. The kookaburra then thrashes its head around, smashing the prey against the ground, its perch, or another hard surface. The bird will even drop prey to the ground to make it more tender. That way the kookaburra can eat it whole. Not bad table manners if you're a bird!

CHAPTER 7

GURGLE AND SLURP

"You do realize that there would have been snakes if we had gone the other way, too," Russell told Eliza. They had been ambling through the dark for over an hour. Russell followed their newest teammate, who seemed to have a one-track mind.

"Yes," she answered. "But I also realize that taking a shortcut is a big risk, especially at night. We're way more likely to stumble into a snake out here. They could be resting in piles of dead leaves or tree stumps, or in the cracks of rocks." She paused to take a drink from her canteen. "They can fall out of trees, too, you know."

"Mmm-hmm," was Russell's reply. He was getting a little sick of the lectures, but he scanned the leafy ceiling of their path for dangling reptiles, just in case.

Sage was up ahead with Dev. They constantly checked the map on the ancam. Occasionally, Sage would make the whole team stop so she could listen to see if other Wild Life teams were on the same trail.

The darkness slowed them down. Every step required caution. But she knew that it gave them one big advantage. In the light of day, Sage would never be able to keep Mari from stopping and swooning over all the marvels and amazing creatures of this exotic land. The darkness meant they were making steady progress, yet she worried they were already too late. "Shhhh. What was that?"

The team came to a halt. "Is it coming from the ground?" Sage wondered out loud as she knelt down. It was a slushing, gurgling sound. There was something about it that Sage did not like. "Anyone know what that is?"

"I'm pretty sure it's giant earthworms sliding through the mud underground," Eliza said, her tone suddenly lighthearted now that they weren't discussing snakes. "They're kind of crazy actually. They can be, like, six feet long. They look like regular worms, but they're just huge."

The rest of the team stared at the ground as the sucky, slurping sound grew louder.

"You don't have to worry about them," Eliza tried to reassure the team. "They only come above ground if super hard rains force them out of their tunnels."

"Um, maybe not, but we *should* worry about this." Dev held up the ancam.

UPDATE: 5 of 6 teams checked in.

"What?" Sage cried. "Only six teams? They're trimming the field *now*?"

Suddenly the slurp of giant earthworms did not seem all that interesting. "We've got to move!" Sage yelled, grabbing Mari's wrist. "This way!"

With a sudden surge of energy, everyone began to race downhill along the creek bed. The echo of the gurgling earthworms still pounded in Sage's head. She and Dev didn't check the ancam or stop to listen for other teams, they just found a steep path and went as fast as they could. Every few minutes, Sage glanced back to make sure they had the whole gang: Dev, Mari, Eliza, Russell, and Jace.

"Did you . . . do this . . . in the last race?" Eliza called out between huffs.

Sage's mind was not on the last race. She was thinking only of this one. There was only one slot left, and soon it would be gone. As they made their way down the sloping ridge, the streambed seemed to grow. Here, it rushed with water.

"Look! An emu!" Mari yelled. "It's gigantic! Easily the second largest bird species in the world."

"Keep moving," Sage begged, not even turning around. Of course Mari, the animal lover, wanted to slow down and take it all in, but there wasn't time. Sage's feet slid beneath her on a patch of wet, slick leaves, and her hiking boots slipped right out from under her, but she pushed herself back up and moved on. As soon as she reached the foot of the hill, she knew why. A tour bus with its headlights on was parked on a narrow paved road just past the edge of the forest. And when Sage looked up the road, she noticed tiny pricks of light. Headlamps.

She rushed back to the edge of the trees. "Run! Fast! We're here!" she yelped. "But so is another team!" Sage suspected that other team had just finished a leisurely boat ride. They probably had lots of energy.

Even as she stood there, Sage could see that darkness was fading. The bus's engine groaned, breaking the hush of twilight. Sage's anxious gaze moved from the bus, to the forest, to the band of approaching headlamps.

"Hurry!" she called. As Dev appeared Sage motioned him toward the bus. "Thank goodness," she muttered when Eliza showed up close behind. Next was Jace, who stopped to wait with Sage.

"They're almost here," he said, his voice revealing unexpected concern. "They'll make it."

The beams of light were now bobbing in the dark. The other team was running.

Sage stepped back to the edge of the forest and peered inside. It was still all shadows. Then Russell burst out, grasping Mari's hand.

"Run!" she demanded. "To the bus!"

Their feet sloshed in the soggy mud. Jace was in step right behind them.

Sage could see Dev and Eliza standing by the bus. The race organizers weren't letting them on. The whole team had to be there.

"Team Ten, checking in," Jace announced when they were still ten steps away. "The final team has arrived," a woman wearing a poncho yelled to the bus driver as everyone climbed aboard.

Their wet soles squeaked on the floor as the bus door folded shut behind them.

Sage took the first seat, collapsing into the soft, dry cushion. As the bus began to pull away, she glanced out the window, and watched as the woman in the poncho had to break the bad news to the next team. Team Ten was officially in the top six and had escaped elimination . . . and bizarre, oversized worms!

CREATURE FEATURE

GIANT EARTHWORM

SCIENTIFIC NAME: *Digaster longmani*

TYPE: invertebrate

RANGE: eastern Australian rain forests

FOOD: organic matter

The giant earthworm has a lot in common with any earthworm you will find in your local park or backyard. It is an invertebrate, which means it does not have a skeleton inside its body like a snake, or a hard skeleton outside its body like an insect. It relies on its muscles to keep its shape, which makes it very fragile. And it uses the bristles along its body to help it move.

Earthworms do not have lungs. Instead, they breathe through their skin. To do this, they need to stay moist at all times. While they do not have a heart, they have five aortic arches, which work to pump blood throughout their body.

Unlike your average earthworm, the giant earthworm rarely comes above ground. It stays several feet under the surface where it is less likely to become dry. It only leaves if a hard rain floods its tunnel system. Also unlike your average earthworm, the giant earthworm can measure over six feet long and can be as wide as a garden hose. It takes it a long time to grow that long, about five years.

CHAPTER 8
RED HOT, BONE-DRY

The sun was rising, and no one had slept. Only six teams remained. Those on the bus were headed to the next stage of the race; everyone else was left behind.

There were plenty of things for the team to talk about, but plenty more reasons to rest.

"If we don't have a new clue, our priority should be sleep," Sage said, tugging a dry fleece from her backpack. She wadded up the jacket and tucked it between her shoulder and her chin. "Wake me if anything shows up on that ancam," she said as she closed her eyes.

She was vaguely aware of Jace shaking her awake and leading everyone across a small runway to a plane whose propeller was already spinning. She was alert long enough to make sure everyone had made the move from bus to small plane. She then put her fleece back in place and fell asleep again.

Hours later, when Sage woke up, her dreams seemed to linger: stars streaming through the sky; snakes skimming the surface of streams; animals changing into people and back again. Sage could hardly be sure she was awake, until Dev leaned over her seat. "We're landing," he said, and he placed the ancam in her hands. She forced herself to blink twice and read:

```
Warm-blooded
Egg layer.
Short-beaked
Insect eater.
Spiny-haired
Milk maker.
```

Sage rubbed her eyes and tried again. Yep, she had read the clue right. She turned around and looked at Dev through the gap between the seats. "Do you have an idea?" she asked hopefully. "Even a teeny tiny inkling?"

"Not really," he replied. "And the clue decoders

are still snoozing." He motioned to Mari and Eliza's seats across the aisle.

Russell pushed his head into view, too. "Do we think this is just one animal?" he questioned in a whisper.

Sage knew what he meant. The lines didn't really go together. The first two lines sounded like some kind of bird, but the last two seemed more like a mammal. "The closest thing I can think of is the platypus."

As if *platypus* were a magic word, Mari sat up looking rested and bright. "What about a platypus?"

"Shhh," Dev reminded her. The nearest team sat several rows behind them, and although it was nearly impossible to hear anything over the

drone of the engines, they couldn't be too careful. He handed the ancam to Mari.

Mari studied the device and moved her finger down the screen as she read each line of the clue. "Don't worry, guys," she said after a moment. "I got this." With a triumphant glance at the still sleeping Eliza, Mari passed the ancam back to Dev and refused to say anything else.

Since they were the last team to board the bus, they were the last team to get off the plane. Javier tipped his hat to them as he left with Team Nine. Dallas and his teammates were in second place.

As she watched all the teams go by, Sage wondered how they had managed it. How had they answered the first two clues so quickly and been the first five teams to make it to the bus? Of course, they'd had boats. They'd had it easy. She wondered if any of the other teams would have blazed their own trail through the thick of a rain forest. How many of their teammates would have agreed to a desperate shortcut in the last dark hours of night?

"If there are only six teams left, are we still Team Ten?" Russell wondered out loud. " 'Cause that's weird."

What Russell said sounded like impossible math, Sage was still so tired.

"Yeah, I liked it better when we were just Team Red," Dev added.

"Yeah, except I was never on Team Red," Eliza reminded them now that she was awake.

"No, you weren't," Mari confirmed.

As soon as the team in fifth place had left

the plane, Eliza turned to her new teammates. "I know you talked about the clue when I was asleep," she announced. "Can you at least let me read it?" Her T-shirt was rumpled and muddy, but she still sat up straight, with her school-picture posture and smile.

Dev reached for the ancam.

As Eliza concentrated on the screen, Mari began to fill in the rest of the team. "You were about as close as you could get, guessing the platypus," she began, a thrill building in her voice. "The answer is a mammal that lays eggs, and there are two animals that do. But the correct answer is not the platypus, it's the other one."

"The echidna," Eliza chimed in, seeming to sit even straighter in her airplane seat. She handed the ancam back to Dev.

"Yes, the echidna," Mari agreed, but she said nothing more.

"The echidna has spines. It is sometimes called the spiny anteater," Eliza informed the team.

"Gather up," Jace announced when the race organizer gave him the cue. "It's our turn."

The desert heat slammed into Sage as the team finally clanged down the airplane steps. They had flown from the wet rain forests of Australia's eastern coast to the center of the continent, where the air was dry and the dirt was red.

One lone Jeep waited for them, parked next to the runway.

"At least this time we've got a ride," said Dev.

"It's good you guys all got some sleep," Jace said as he tossed his hiking pack in the Jeep.

"Finding this one could take a while." He got in and then took a long look in the rearview mirror as the team got settled in. "Eliza, you coming?"

Everyone else had climbed into the Jeep, but Eliza was bent down next to the door, examining the vehicle's floor. "Sure thing," she said. "Just checking for extra passengers."

For some reason, Sage had thought that Eliza's snake obsession would end when they left the rain forest, but apparently not.

Once Eliza's door slammed shut, Jace asked for directions.

The original members of Team Red looked to Mari.

"Um, I don't know," she answered. "The echidna lives pretty much anywhere it can find food. It eats termites and ants, which doesn't really help us narrow in on a spot to start searching."

Sage gazed out at the endless expanse of flat land and low shrubs. "We can't just wander around. This place is endless!"

"Well, it's still the hottest part of the day," Eliza said. "The books say that the echidna hunts when it's cooler. Morning and later afternoon. Some might not even come out until night. I don't think we want to wait."

Sage had purposely left the seat next to her open for Eliza. She really needed her team to work together. They were in last place, and the other teams were super-speedy.

"I got something," Dev mumbled as he checked the team's device. "They just sent us a starting point. I think we're going on a hike."

Sage was flooded with relief. A hike would be good for the team, would give them direction. By the end of their last race in Africa, Team Red had a rhythm, and everyone played their part. Now Eliza had joined their team. Sage knew their new teammate could play a part, too. She just didn't know what that part was yet.

"Into the Outback!" Russell declared, and the Jeep rumbled down the open road.

MYSTERIOUS MONOTREMES

PLATYPUS

ECHIDNA

They lay eggs! And they are mammals! They're amazing! They're monotremes!

There are only five living monotreme species. One is a platypus. The other four are echidnas.

The platypus is such an odd creature that the scientists who first examined it thought it was some kind of trick. What would you think of a duck-billed, beaver-tailed, web-footed, egg-laying animal? You might not believe it was a mammal. But the platypus has hair. It also produces milk for its young. These are the main features that make it a mammal.

Echidnas also have hair and produce milk. And they look a bit like more familiar animals, such as porcupines and hedgehogs. However, like the platypus, echidnas lay eggs. This means echidnas are also monotremes—mammals that lay eggs.

When reptile eggs hatch, the babies are able to move and find food on their own.

Monotreme babies are different. Much like a marsupial baby, they are only the size of a bean. They will need to drink their mother's milk for several months before they are ready to leave the burrow to find food of their own.

The platypus lives only in Australia. Echidnas live in Australia, but they are also found in New Guinea.

CHAPTER 9

WALKABOUT

"**W**here are the other teams?" Sage asked as Jace pulled up to a single Wild Life flag. The pole stood crooked in the middle of a vast and dusty landscape. "The last team should only have had a five-minute lead on us, right? Shouldn't we be able to see them?"

"Not necessarily," Jace responded. "The organizers might have given them a different starting spot." Then, anticipating the team's complaints, he added, "Their start won't be any closer to the next checkpoint than yours. The organizers just want each team to have its own path."

Sage frowned. The same thing had happened in the rain forest, and she didn't think it was fair. It was a race! Everyone should have the same course!

"So, where are we going? What's our destination?" Eliza asked.

"Check the ancam," Jace suggested. "If you have one, it will be there."

"Nothing," Dev said, strapping the device back in place. "Nada. Zip. Zilch."

"It's a walkabout," Mari said. "I read about them in one of the airport brochures. It's when native Australians go on a journey in the wilderness."

Sage thought this hardly seemed like the time

to wander around. "No, it's not a walkabout!" she yelled, all the nerves in her arms and legs twitching. "It's a race! We just don't know where we're going!"

The heat blazed down on the team. Everyone seemed to study the dusty ground.

"But we do have a clue," Mari said. "Sure, echidnas could be anywhere, but we can still look for one. They might be hiding from the heat under rocks or in hollows."

"So could snakes," Eliza pointed out.

"They'll be searching for insects. They're about this high . . ." Mari kneeled down and held her hand several inches from the cracked ground.

"Mari's right," Russell said. "We know how to do this, so let's go."

Sage watched as the team headed out, search-ing for echidnas in the bush. She snapped on her hiking pack and followed.

Sage had picked up that the "bush" was a term for wild country. In Australia, it was especially used for the open plains. It seemed a lot like the savanna in Africa, except for the animals. Australia didn't have giant herds of antelopes and zebras. There also weren't any large carnivores, like lions, cheetahs, and leopards. Here, dingos were the largest predators.

As far as she remembered, it wasn't totally clear how or when the wild dogs showed up in Australia. They had probably come from Asia over 3,000 years ago, and they lived in packs like wolves. Sage knew dingos were rarely a threat to humans. They were incredible hunters with exceptional hearing, but they focused on smaller prey like rabbits, lizards, and rodents. Still, Sage stayed alert.

Eliza had her eyes out for another threat. "You know, the king brown snake is insanely venom- ous. It's not highly toxic, but it carries nearly five times the venom of other snakes. It doesn't even live in the rain forest. We're more likely to run into it out here." Her eyes darted from side to side as the team spread out to cover more ground.

Sage's concern only grew after they had spent over two hours walking around aimlessly. Finding a small mammal in an endless desert was not easy. This was a race, and yet they were slowly scouring the ground. It made no sense to Sage. At least the heat lifted when the sun started to go down.

They were nearing a formation of large rocks. It looked like a crumbled wall, but Sage knew it was natural. It wasn't too high. The team could go around it, but it would be faster—if not easier—to climb.

"Is everyone up for it?" Jace asked. "Do you have enough light?"

Sage looked around at her teammates. No one was eager to do this—especially Eliza—but they all knew it could save valuable time, so they agreed. As they grasped for handholds, Sage could hear Eliza muttering to herself. Sage knew from Eliza's earlier lectures that the rocks would be a prime place for snakes.

"Do you want to follow me?" Sage asked. "If we take the same path, we'll be less likely to disturb anything." Eliza didn't answer, but she scooted over so she was behind the team leader.

When they reached the crest, Mari drew in a momentous breath. Just below them, a mob of kangaroos clustered under a group of trees.

The sky blushed in the twilight. In the distance, they could see a giant brick-red rock rising from the flat surface of the desert. It had two names: the newer name, Ayer's Rock, and the name given to it by the people who had lived in the area for thousands of years, Uluru.

Sage could tell why the Aboriginal Australians, the people native to the land, considered the great mass of sandstone sacred. It seemed to

rise from deep in the earth, powerful and impressive.

"I feel like I'm really in Australia now," Mari whispered, taking it all in. The kangaroos nibbled tall, dry grass. Several joeys peeked out from pouches. The adults leaned on their front legs, and then rocked their powerful hind legs forward as they moved from one tuft of grass to another.

Sage allowed Mari a moment before she reminded them all that there was a race to run.

After they skidded down the other side of the rock, Mari wanted to inspect the nooks and crannies at the bottom. "This is a perfect place for echidnas to hide," she explained. "It would be shady during the day, and I'll bet there are tons of insects. If I were an echidna, I'd like it here." She got down on her hands and knees for a better view, but Jace insisted she use a torch, just in case. Most animals—even the dangerous ones—would shy away from the flames.

Eliza didn't think it was a good idea, until Mari found the nest. "It's got to be an echidna burrow. I'll bet the echidna didn't go far," Mari thought out loud.

Sage had them spread out to search, but the hunt didn't last long.

"Oh, it's so cute," Eliza cooed when she spotted the spiky creature. "Dev, come quick!"

Dev came running with his trigger finger already in position on the ancam. The five teammates crowded around as the echidna used its tough claws to dig deep in its search for termites.

"Its face looks like a hedgehog," Dev said.

"Its spines look like a porcupine," suggested Russell.

"Its tongue is like an anteater," said Eliza.

"Its claws look like a badger," offered Sage.

"But it isn't really related to any of those," Mari said. "Its closest relative is the platypus, which has a bill like a duck and a tail like a beaver."

Once again, Sage thought about the different strengths and weaknesses of her teammates. "Whatever it takes to get the job done," she said.

No one had a response to that, so they stood and stared at the ancam. They needed their next clue.

CREATURE FEATURE

RED KANGAROO

SCIENTIFIC NAME: *Macropus rufus*

TYPE: mammal

RANGE: dry climates in central Australia

FOOD: grasses and leaves

The red kangaroo is one of four species of full-size kangaroos, and it is the largest of all marsupials. It is also one of the most successful. While dingos might target young joeys or older adults, healthy red kangaroos do not have animal predators.

A kangaroo's hind legs are large and powerful, with long, padded feet to help propel it in its mighty hops. A large kangaroo can reach a speed of nearly forty miles per hour, with hops as long as twenty-six feet and as high as nine. Of course, hops of four to six feet make for a more relaxed pace. Fun fact: A kangaroo cannot walk! If it wants to move at a slower rate, it has to use its tail like a fifth leg. Balancing its weight on its tail and short front legs, it swings its hind legs forward in a rocking motion.

Kangaroos have a lot of marsupial cousins in Australia and neighboring islands. Wallaroos are medium-sized and wallabies are much smaller, but all share the classic kangaroo traits. Several species of tree kangaroos exist as well. While they are shorter than their land-dwelling relatives and have longer front legs, they still have long feet, a forward-leaning posture, and, of course, a pouch!

CHAPTER 10

MULTIPLE CHOICE

It seemed like they had been waiting for the clue forever. Sage held up the torch and glanced around. They had made progress, heading toward Uluru, but the monumental rock still appeared so far away. In Sage's mind, Uluru was their obvious destination. She was certain that was where the race organizers were sending them. "Anything yet?" she asked Dev.

"Not yet," he replied.

"Everyone, take a drink," Sage prompted, trying to keep the team ready and herself busy. In the flickering torchlight, she regarded her teammates. They stood in a loose circle, not too far away from one another, but not too close.

"Here it is," Dev said, setting down his canteen so he could read.

Which two animals play a role in a native creation myth about the formation of Uluru?

A. The kangaroo and the koala
B. The dingo and the sheep
C. The mulga and the carpet python
D. None of the above

Eliza said what they were all thinking. "Multiple choice? Seriously?"

Sage was confused. There was no prompt to get a picture. No riddle. Was it a trick? Was Bull Gordon trying to catch them off guard?

"No way is it the dingo and the sheep," Russell said. "Sheep didn't even live here until people arrived from Europe. The myth would be way older than that."

Sage nodded. That made a lot of sense.

"I question the kangaroo and the koala," Dev added. "Remember what Mari said? The koala doesn't live around here. I kind of doubt it would be in the myth."

"That eliminates the first two," Sage said. "What about the third one?" When no one answered anything, Sage asked, "Do we think it's none of the above?"

After a moment, Eliza took a deep breath and clasped her hands. "I actually think the third one is right," she said. "The mulga is another name for the king brown snake. I probably don't need to say that I've read a lot about snakes. It's one way I deal with how much I'm afraid of them. Anyway, I remember once reading a story about Uluru. Ancient spirits transformed into snakes and fought one another. Their battle was epic, and people say you can see marks on the side of Uluru that tell the tale."

Something about Eliza's explanation seemed familiar to Sage.

"But do you know it was the mulga and the

carpet python?" Dev asked. "They could be trying to trick us."

"I can't be positive," Eliza said. "I think those are the right ones, but I'm honestly better at remembering details about fangs and venom."

"You *are* excellent at that," Russell said.

Sage had a good feeling about it. She thought they should go with Eliza's answer, but it wasn't just her decision. "So," she began, "this is a race. We should probably submit an answer soon."

"Eliza knows more about snakes than anyone I've ever met," Mari said matter-of-factly. "I trust her instincts."

"Me, too," Russell added.

"And me," was Dev's reply.

"So we all agree," Sage said. "Let's do it."

The reply was almost immediate:

Congratulations! Your team will
move on to compete in the next leg
of the race.

"We're in!" Mari gasped with delight. "Eliza, that was all you."

"Yeah, good work. You're like a snake scholar," said Dev.

"I'm happy to help," Eliza said with a smile. And for once, Sage noted, it was not that staged, school-picture smile.

"That's it?" Russell looked puzzled. "Can they do that? Can they just message us and then leave us here in the Outback? No big race to the finish, no big feast with other teams at the end?"

Sage understood Russell's confusion. In the past, the race courses always ended with a big moment. But Sage wasn't sure they needed that this time. "It doesn't seem like a bad thing, spending time with just the team," she suggested as she looked around at everyone. They all had red dust smeared across their faces and ground into their nails.

"Yeah, I don't really care about the other teams," Russell admitted, "but I seriously need some food."

"I'm good with staying here," Mari said. She tilted her head back and stared up at the stars.

Jace had begun unpacking the contents of his pack. He set out a blanket, stacked a small batch of kindling, and produced a pile of food, with the makings of s'mores on top.

"This doesn't look like a well-rounded meal," Dev pointed out.

"Maybe not, but it'll tide you over for now," Jace replied. "We have to do something to celebrate your making it to the next stage." He stood up and began to gather kindling for a fire. "Javier told me you guys were solid. He thought you had a good chance to win it all."

Sage smiled and sat down on the blanket. She was happy to not have to be the leader for a while. Maybe it could be nice if Eliza—or anyone else, really—wanted to step up and make decisions now and again. Sage decided that it wouldn't be so bad if they didn't have specific roles all the time. It turned out they all were good at lots of things. Dev was great with the ancam, but he also picked up on things that others didn't. Russell was a natural athlete, but he was also good at motivating the team. Mari knew tons of facts,

but she was also a calming force. And although Sage hadn't realized it at first, Eliza wasn't just a walking textbook. She had good instincts. Maybe coming together as a team meant they could rely on one another to help out when things weren't going the way they'd planned, to share roles and responsibilities. Except when it came to snakes. Eliza would always be their snake expert. No one else wanted that job.

"So what's next?" Dev said, double-checking the ancam screen for updates. "What do we do?"

"Maybe we should hike to Uluru," Mari said, "after we rest. We could look for the battle scene of the spirit snakes." Mari stared at the silhouette of the great rock. A dingo howl carried over the flat land. Another came as a reply.

"I don't like it," Eliza admitted, but she wasn't talking about the hike to Uluru, or the dingos, or even the snakes. "The next leg of the race could start at any time. And here we are, roasting s'mores? We should be preparing."

"For now, all we can do is wait," said Jace.

Sage smiled to herself. She and Eliza had a lot in common. Sage was anxious to get started again, too. The race wasn't over. They had only come to a stopping point. When would the next stage start? Where would they go? Which other teams were still in the competition?

Sage shook her head. She was learning that she wasn't good at waiting for answers. Luckily, she was excellent at making s'mores.

Want to know what happens when *The Wild Life*

heads to the Himalayan mountains? Read on for

a glimpse of the next race course in

The tingling seemed to start in Russell's nose, but it also stretched to his toes and fingers. He clenched his hands into fists and buried them in the pockets of his jacket.

"I'm not that cold," Dev announced, looking at the rugged peaks above. The mountains rose in jagged steps, each taller than the next. The highest ones were crusted with layers of pure white ice and snow. "I shouldn't be cold, right? It's spring. So why are my hands numb?"

"The higher we go, the colder it gets," Eliza reminded them. "The Himalayas are the highest mountains in the world, you know."

"But that tingling probably isn't from cold," Maya chimed in. "It could be from a lack of good air. The higher we go, the less oxygen there is."

"Well, yeah," Eliza added between shallow puffs. "Obviously."

Mari was talking about altitude sickness. Russell knew it was no joke. Not getting enough oxygen could make you very sick. His mom had told him about it after watching a movie. She had said that it started with a tingling, itchy feeling in the hands and feet, and it could cause dizziness and nausea. Russell knew that if he didn't feel better soon, it could sideline him. It could knock any of them out of the race.

"We've been climbing for a while," Sage said to the team. "Maybe we should take a break." Sage was the group's de facto leader. For Russell, Mari, and Dev, it was their sixth race with Sage, and they all had come to rely on her. She looked out for them, and not necessarily just for their chances to win. But they all knew the truth: Sage did not like to come in second.

But this time, Russell did not agree with their leader. He preferred to keep moving. As long as he was taking steps, searching for safe footing, his mind wouldn't wander to other things. After all, there were a *lot* of other things to think about. Some of the teams had already been eliminated. No one knew which teams were still in it, but Russell was willing to bet that his old friend Dallas and the rest of Team Nine had made the cut. Russell just had a feeling, and not necessarily a good one.

"Can you check the ancam again, Dev?" Eliza asked. "It's hard to believe we've hiked all this way, and the race organizers haven't given us a single clue. It seems like a waste of time and energy."

"I just checked the ancam, like, two minutes

ago," Dev assured them, patting the trusty communication unit. Dev kept it strapped to his chest in a handcrafted harness, so he could grab it in two seconds flat (1.63 seconds to be precise). Dev took his job of operating the gadget, which was their only connection to the race organizers, very seriously.

"Can you check again?" Eliza prompted.

After a moment, Dev answered Eliza. "The ancam still doesn't show anything except the X on the map. I think we should keep going. We aren't far." Dev glanced at the flame-colored sun as it dropped lower in the sky. "We might not be really cold now, but that'll change as soon as the sun goes behind one of the mountains."

"And spotting animals in the dark won't get any easier," Mari noted. That was the whole point of *The Wild Life* after all. The race was an around-the-world competition—in some of the planet's most remote places—to seek out animals and animal facts. Russell knew Mari was right. She usually was when it came to the animals. Nightfall would make tracking any wildlife more difficult . . . and more dangerous.

Russell took as deep a breath as his lungs would allow. "I agree. Let's keep moving," he panted. He was exhausted and needed to rest, but he wanted to get to their designated stopping point before he collapsed.

Over his heavy breath, he heard a howl ring out. Seconds later, another howl joined it. This one was long and high, like a siren.

"Is that what I think it was?" Russell wondered out loud.

"I think so," Eliza answered.

Another howl carried through the cool, crisp air.

"On second thought, we should keep going," Sage said.

"Good thinking," Dev answered, picking up the pace.

"It's probably the wolves in a pack calling to one another, trying to meet back up," Mari said, sounding unconcerned.

"Or maybe they are warning another pack to stay out of their way," Eliza added in a matter-of-fact tone.

"Does it matter why they're howling?" Russell asked. "There are wolves close by. Too close for comfort."

"Don't be so sure," Mari replied. "Wolf howls can carry over six miles."

Six miles was far, but Russell was sure those calls were from much closer.

"I can see a light up ahead!" Dev called. "I'll bet it's our rest stop."

Russell searched the path in front of them until he saw the glimmer of a lantern. Then he looked back, past Eliza and their chaperone, Jace. He thought he could see the silhouette of a wolf on a cliff in the distance. Moments later, a mournful howl sounded, and Russell knew the wolves weren't far behind.

READ *MOUNTAIN MISSION* TO FIND OUT WHAT HAPPENS NEXT!

JOIN THE RACE!

It's an incredible adventure through the animal kingdom, as kids zip-line, kayak, and scuba dive their way to the finish line! Packed with cool facts about amazing creatures, dangerous habitats, and more!

SCHOLASTIC

scholastic.com

I SURVIVED

Find out how a kid could survive
the greatest disasters in history!

Read the bestselling series by Lauren Tarshis!

Available in print and eBook editions

Test your survival skills at **scholastic.com/isurvived**

■ SCHOLASTIC